Gibraltar

DISCOVER INTRIGUING FACTS
CHILDREN'S PEOPLE AND PLACES BOOK

Located on the southern tip of Spain, Gibraltar is a British Overseas Territory. It is dominated by the Rock of Gibraltar, a 416m high limestone ridge.

The Rock was first settled by the Moors during the Middle Ages. Later it was ruled by Spain and finally given to the British in 1713. Some interesting Gibraltar Facts include the Great Siege Tunnels, which were expanded during World War II.

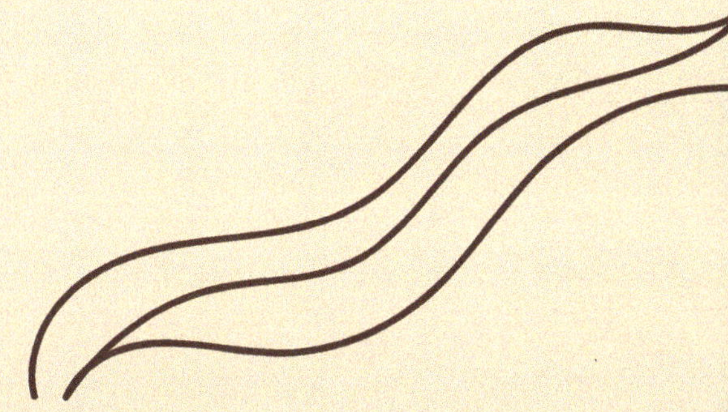

GIBRALTAR IS LOCATED AT THE END OF SPAIN

Gibraltar is located at the southern tip of the Iberian Peninsula, bordering Spain to the north. Since 1713, it has been a British Overseas Territory.

In 2002, a referendum held on the country's future decided that ninety-eight percent of Gibraltarians wanted to stay British. Due to its strategic location at the mouth of the Mediterranean, Gibraltar has seen a rise in international trade and financial services. Formerly a crucial naval base and military outpost, Gibraltar has evolved into a leading financial services center.

IT HAS A MEDITERRANEAN CLIMATE

Gibraltar has a Mediterranean climate, which means that the weather is generally pleasant year-round. Summers are warm and dry, and the winters are mild. The sunshine hours are high, and temperatures rarely fall below 30°C.

The climate in Gibraltar is influenced by two prevailing winds: the easterly Levante, which originates from the Sahara in Africa, and the westerly Wind, which is more temperate and provides crisper air. The climate is generally mild and pleasant, and the weather is generally sunny, but it can be rainy, especially during the winter.

Gibraltar is a British Overseas Territory. It borders Spain on the west and faces Africa in the north. Its rocky mountain makes it a popular location for tourists, and it has developed into an important maritime transport point.

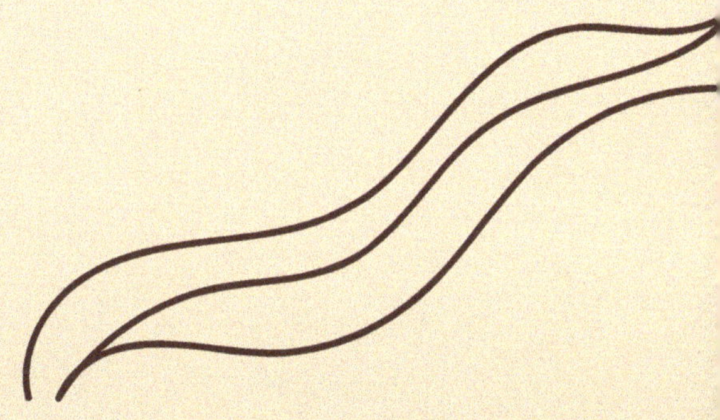

Although the territory has its own government and a large population, Britain retains responsibility for foreign relations and defence.

IT HAS OVER 130 CAVES

The ancient Neanderthals of Gibraltar lived in caves in Gibraltar. An engraving discovered in one of the Gibraltar caves dates back 39,100 years, and suggests that the inhabitants of Gorham's Cave had a skill for symbolic thinking.

These caves were also home to many predators and prey, such as hyenas. The engraving was found during excavations of a small ledge located about 320 feet inside the cave.

Gibraltar is home to more than 100 caves, many of which are accessible by foot. The caves were used by the Neanderthals when the sea levels were much lower. They shared their habitat with a much wider variety of birds and animals.

These caves are still full of bird bones, and scientists have found evidence of human processing of the remains. The fossils found here represent more than 30 percent of the European bird species, and many of them show signs of prehistoric processing.

IT HAS A GREEK POPULATION

Gibraltar is a mountain straddling the Mediterranean and the Atlantic Ocean. The Greeks called it Calpe and it marked the boundary between the known and unknown world.

In 711, the Islamic governor of Tangier landed at Gibraltar, launching an invasion of the Iberian Peninsula. Gibraltar then took the name of Jabal Tariq (Mountain of Tariq).

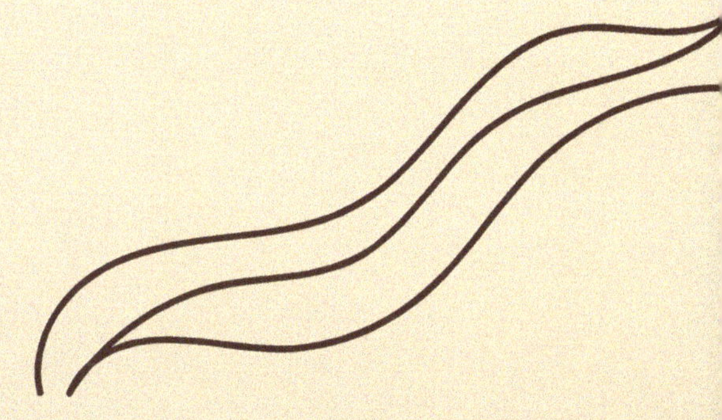

The Gibraltar Straits mark the mixing of the Atlantic and Mediterranean seawaters. The Mediterranean Sea is very salty and dense, and the Atlantic water in the straits pushes it downward.

This causes a recirculating current, which brings different species to Gibraltar.

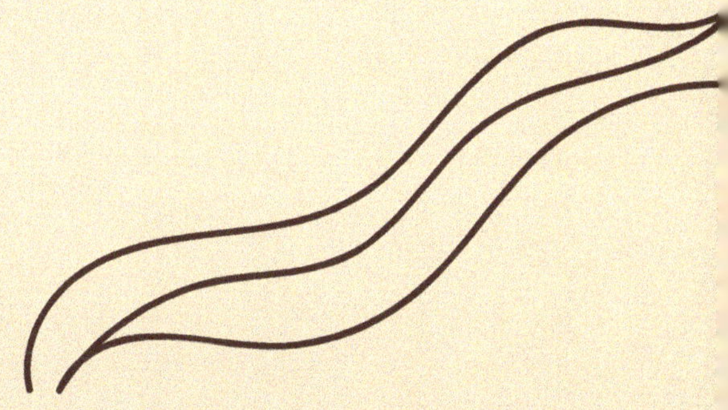

IT HAS A HIGH DENSITY OF PEOPLE

The population of Gibraltar is estimated at 33,812 people as of 1 January 2022. This represents an increase of 0.22 percent from the previous year.

The natural increase in the population was 201, while the number of people living in the country declined by 111 due to external migration.

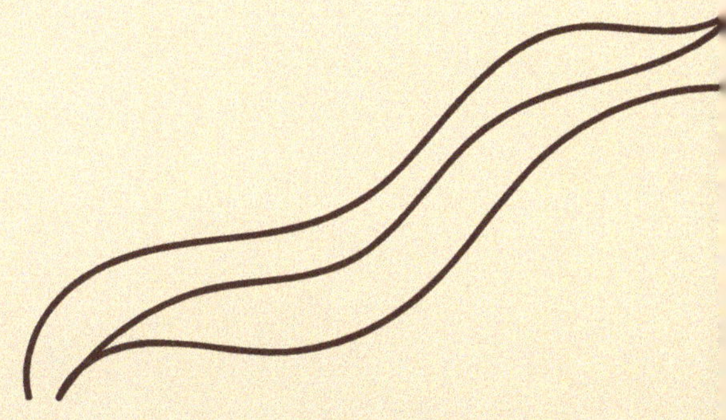

Vaccination of people who live in Gibraltar is a priority. Since the number of residents living in Gibraltar is very high, it is important to ensure that everyone in the community is protected.

The government has implemented strict vaccination guidelines for the region and is working on a contingency plan to top up vaccination rates in Gibraltar.

IT HAS A LOCAL LANGUAGE

Gibraltar has a local language that is very distinct from the other Spanish-speaking areas of Spain. The main dialect, known as Llanito, is a mixture of Spanish and British English, with over 500 words of Genoese origin.

Although English is the official language, many locals also speak Llanito. There are even a number of dialects and dialectal variations.

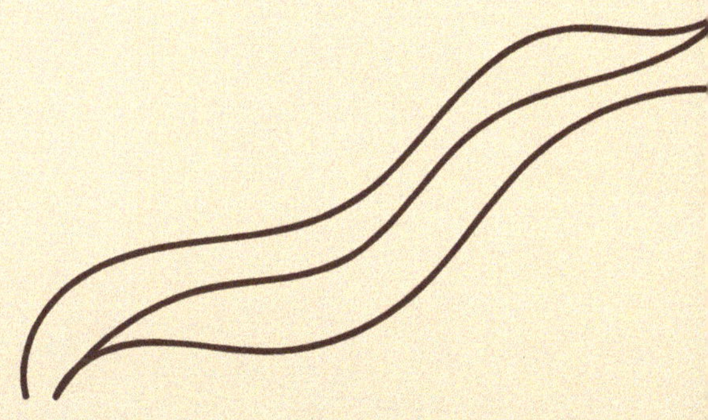

Gibraltar is an island off the southern tip of Spain with a population of around thirty thousand people. The official language is English, but Gibraltarians speak Spanish and Arabic, the languages of the island's neighbours.

Other languages that are widely spoken include Portuguese, Italian, and Russian. Most Gibraltarians are Roman Catholic, but there are also groups of Protestants, Muslims, and Jews living in the territory.

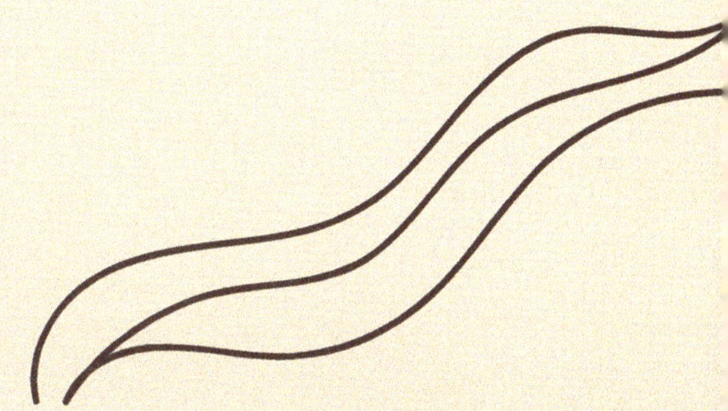